This Book
Belongs to

_____

Parrots, Pirates and Walking the Plank

© 1992 by Educational Publishing Concepts, Inc., Wheaton, IL
Exclusive Distribution by Chariot Books

Library of Congress Cataloging-in-Publication Data
Hollingworth, Mary
        Parrots, pirates, and walking the plank : a book about obeying /
Mary Hollingsworth.
            lc.- cm.
        Summary: Hearing the story of Jonah from his friend Uncle Elzy convinces Jeff of the importance of obedience to his parents and to God.
        ISBN 0-7814-0668-4
        [1. Obedience—Fiction. 2. Christian life—Fiction.] I. Title.
PZ7.H72526PAR   1992
[Fic]—dc20

                                                    92-8089
                                                    CIP
Printed in The United States of America.   AC
7 6 5 4 3 2 1   97 96 95 94 93 92

Parrots, Pirates
and
Walking the Plank

"A Book about Obeying"

Written by
Mary Hollingsworth

Illustrated by
Daniel J. Hochstatter

Obey! Obey! And Anchors Aweigh!

Ahoy, ahoy and anchors aweigh!
Oh, children, take heed; your parents obey,
Do what they request with a smile and a song,
And you'll find life's happy as you go along.

Now, hear me, my maties, and do what I say—
It usually pays off just to simply obey,
For when you refuse (I have to be frank),
You might have to pay by walking the plank!

—Uncle Elzy

"Ahoy there!" shouted Jeff. Then he clanged the big ship's bell that stood by the front door.

"Who goes there?" called a deep, friendly voice from inside the big, old house that looked out on Hargrave Harbor.

"It's First Mate Jeff, Sir," said Jeff. "Permission to come aboard?"

"Permission granted, Matey. I'm in the living quarters."

Jeff found his friend Uncle Elzy, a retired sea captain, in the living room happily whistling and cleaning his parrot's cage. Captain Stash, the old tomcat, was asleep on the rug.

"Here come the pirates! Here come the pirates!" squawked Jibber Jabber as Jeff came in.

"Well, shiver me timbers, Matey," said Uncle Elzy. "What brings you aboard?"

Jeff climbed up in Uncle Elzy's favorite old chair and sat down. "I'm not going back, Sir," said Jeff. "My mom always makes me clean my room on Saturday. I hate cleaning my room. That's girl stuff! So, I ran away."

"Well, blow me down," said Uncle Elzy. "You know, I heard of another swabbie who ran away one time. Why, he almost got a whole ship's crew drowned!"

"Really?" asked Jeff. "What happened?"

"Hit the deck! Hit the deck!"
yelled Jibber Jabber.

Uncle Elzy laughed and sat down.
"Now, let's see," he said. "The way I
heard it, the ship took on some cargo and a
passenger named Jonah at Joppa.

Then they set sail for Tarshish. The sailors were swabbing the deck and polishing the brass when a terrible storm hit them. The waves were crashing so hard the old ship creaked. They thought she was going to come apart for sure."

"Then what happened?" Jeff asked.

"Batten the hatches! Batten the hatches!" squawked the bird.

13

"The crew was afraid," said Uncle Elzy. "They were so scared they threw all the cargo into the sea. That way the ship would be lighter and might not sink into the briney deep. But it didn't help. The storm was so bad that it just tossed the ship around like a toothpick."

"Wow!" said Jeff. "Then what?"

"Finally the crew got below deck. That fellow Jonah was lying there sound asleep. He'd slept through the whole storm! They couldn't believe it."

"What did they do?" asked Jeff.

"Walk the plank! Walk the plank!" muttered Jibber Jabber.

Uncle Elzy grinned at the bird. "The sailors asked Jonah what he had done to cause such a storm. And you'll never believe it! He said he was running away from God."

"Why?" asked Jeff.

"God had told him to go preach to an evil city called Nineveh. But he didn't want to go. So, he ran away and got on their ship. He said the only way to save the ship was to throw him overboard. Now, they wanted that storm to stop all right. But they didn't want to throw a swabbie in the brink. He'd drown for sure."

"What did they do?" asked Jeff.

"Row, row, row your boat," sang the parrot.

"First, they tried to row the ship to shore. They rowed with all their might for hours and hours. But the storm just got worse and worse."

"They finally did what Jonah told them to do. They threw him right into that stormy sea!"

"Did Jonah drown?" asked Jeff.

23

"Well, not exactly, Mate. You see, this huge fish suddenly came up and swallowed him right down!"

Jeff's eyes grew big as he asked, "Swallowed him?"

24

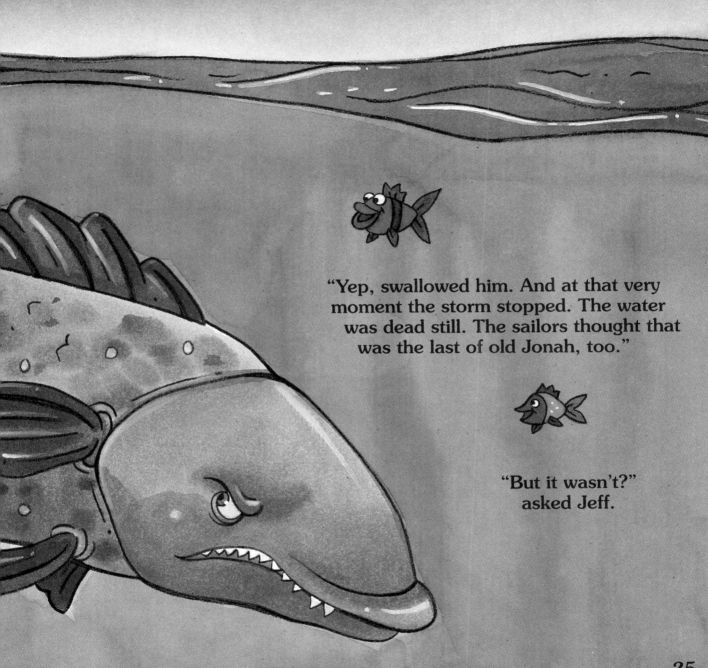

"Yep, swallowed him. And at that very moment the storm stopped. The water was dead still. The sailors thought that was the last of old Jonah, too."

"But it wasn't?" asked Jeff.

"Nope," laughed Uncle Elzy.

"What happened?" asked Jeff.

"Well, Jonah was in the belly of that fish for three whole days and nights. He was scared silly, too. Deep water almost drowned him. Slimy seaweed was wrapped around his head.

He thought he was a goner for sure. He prayed and asked God to save him. Finally, God made that fish just politely spit Jonah out onto the shore. He was safe and sound. Then you know what he did?"

Thinking hard, Jeff said, "I'll bet he went to Nineveh like God had told him to do in the first place."

"That's right, Jeff," said Uncle Elzy with his eyes twinkling.

Suddenly Jeff jumped down off the chair. That surprised Captain Stash, who skittered under the couch. As Jeff ran toward the front door, he said, "Thanks Uncle Elzy! I've got to go now."

"Well, blow me down, Matey. Where are you sailing off to in such a storm?"

"I've got to get home and clean up my room!" said Jeff. "If sailors clean their ship, I guess cleaning isn't just girls' work. Besides, I remember in the Bible that God said we children are supposed to obey our parents. And I don't want to disobey God like Jonah did."

"Squawk! Anchors aweigh! Anchors aweigh!" said Jibber Jabber.

Uncle Elzy chuckled as the front door slammed behind Jeff. Then he went back to whistling and cleaning Jibber Jabber's cage.

"Loving God means obeying his commands. And God's commands are not too hard for us." (I John 5:3, Internatinal Children's Bible).

If you'd like to read more about Jonah, you can find his story in the Bible in Jonah 1—3.